ABSENT FRIENDS

A Play

ALAN AYCKBOURN

SAMUEL   FRENCH

LONDON

NEW YORK   TORONTO   SYDNEY   HOLLYWOOD

ABSENT FRIENDS

First produced at the Library Theatre, Scarborough, on June 17th, 1974, and subsequently at the Garrick Theatre, London, on July 23rd, 1975, with the following cast of characters:

Paul	Peter Bowles
Diana	Pat Heywood
John	Ray Brooks
Evelyn	Cheryl Kennedy
Colin	Richard Briers
Marge	Phyllida Law

The play directed by Eric Thompson
Designed by Derek Cousins

The action takes place in the open-plan living-room of a modern executive-style house

ACT I   Saturday, 3 p.m.
ACT II   Immediately following

Time – the present

ACT I

The open-plan living-room of a modern executive-style house. Saturday, 3 p.m.

The room is primarily furnished with English Swedish-style furniture. A lot of wrought-iron for gates in lieu of doors and as used for room dividers: also artistic frosted glass. Doubtful pictures. A bar. Parquet floor with rugs. It all cost a great deal. Archways lead off to the kitchen and back doors, and to the front door and bedrooms, etc.

When the CURTAIN *rises Evelyn, a heavily made-up, reasonably trendily dressed, expressionless girl is discovered sitting on a bar-stool by a pram which she is absently rocking with one hand, whilst gazing blankly ahead. Near her, on a large coffee table, tea is laid out in the form of sandwiches, cakes and biscuits, under suitable coverings. Only the teapot and hot water jug are missing. Evelyn chews and sings to herself*

After a moment, Diana enters from the kitchen. She takes a cigarette packet from the bench below the fire, finds it empty, and throws it into the fireplace. She takes a packet from her handbag, also on the bench, and lights it with a lighter from the bag. She is older than Evelyn, in her mid to later thirties. She always gives the impression of being slightly strained. She smiles occasionally, but it is painful. Her sharp darting eyes do not miss much after years of suspicions both genuine and unfounded.

Diana Have you got him to sleep?
Evelyn Yes.
Diana (*looking into the pram*) Aaah! They look so lovely like that. Like little cherubims.
Evelyn (*unenthusiastically*) Mmm.
Diana Just like little cherubims. (*Anxiously*) Should he be covered up as much as that, dear?
Evelyn Yes.
Diana Won't he get too hot?
Evelyn He likes it hot.
Diana Oh. I was just worried he wasn't getting enough air.
Evelyn He's all right. He doesn't need much air.
Diana Oh, well . . . (*She looks about her*) Well, I think we're all ready for them. John's on his way, you say?
Evelyn Yes.
Diana How is he these days? I haven't seen John for ages.
Evelyn He's all right.
Diana I haven't seen either of you.
Evelyn We're all right.
Diana Not for ages. Well, I'm glad you could come this afternoon. Colin

really will appreciate that, I'm sure. Seeing us all. (*Pause*) Paul should be home soon. I think he's playing his squash again.
Evelyn Oh.
Diana Him and his squash. It used to be tennis—now he's squash mad. Squash, squash, squash. Can't see what he sees in it. All afternoon hitting a ball against a wall. It's so noisy. Bang, bang, bang. He's not even out of doors. No fresh air at all. It can't be good for him. Does John play squash?
Evelyn No.
Diana Oh.
Evelyn He doesn't play anything.
Diana Oh, well. He probably doesn't need it. Exercise. Some men don't. My father never took a stroke of exercise. Till he died. He seemed fit enough. He managed to do what he wanted to do. Mind you, he never did very much. He just used to sit and shout at we girls. Most of the time. He got calmer though when he got older. After my mother left him. (*Looking into the pram*) Did you knit that little jacket for him?
Evelyn No.
Diana Pretty. (*Pause. During the following she checks and arranges the dishes on the table*) No, there are times when I think that's the principle trouble between Paul and me. I mean, I know now I'm running myself down but Paul basically, he's got much more go—well, I mean let's face it, he's much cleverer than me. Let's face it. Basically. I mean, I was the bright one in our family but I can't keep up with Paul sometimes. When he has one of his moods, I think to myself, now if I was really clever, I could probably talk him round or something but I mean the thing is, really and truly, and I know I'm running myself down when I say this, I don't think I'm really enough for him. He needs me, I can tell that; he doesn't say as much but I know he does. It's just, as I say, I don't think I'm really enough for him. (*She reflects*) But he couldn't do without me. Make no mistake about that. He's got this amazing energy. I don't know where he finds it. He goes to bed long after me, he's up at dawn, working down here—then off he goes all day—I need my eight hours, it's no good. What I'm saying is really, I wouldn't blame him. Not altogether. If he did. With someone else. You know, another woman. I wouldn't blame him, I wouldn't blame her. Not as long as I was told. Providing I know, that I'm told—all right. Providing I feel able to say to people—"Yes, I am well aware that my husband is having an affair with such and such or whoever—it's quite all right. I know all about it. We're both grown-up people, we know what we're doing, he knows I know, she knows I know. So mind your own business." I'd feel all right about it. But I will not stand deception. I'm simply asking that I be told. Either by him or, if not, by her. Not necessarily now but sometime. You see.

Diana goes to the kitchen

Evelyn sits expressionless

Diana returns with an ashtray, which she puts on the bar

I know he is, you see. He's not very clever and he's a very bad liar like most men. If he takes the trouble, like last Saturday, to tell me he's just going down the road to the football match, he might at least choose a day when they're playing at home. (*She lifts the tablecloth and inspects the sandwiches*) I hope I've made enough tomato. No, I must be told. Otherwise it makes my life impossible. I can't talk to anybody without them. . . . I expect them, both of them, at least to have some feeling for me. (*She blows her nose*) Well?

The doorbell rings

Excuse me.

Diana goes out to open the front door

Marge (*off*) Only me.
Diana Marge!
Marge (*off*) I've been shopping. Don't laugh.
Diana Leave your coat?
Marge Oh yes.

There is the sound of shopping bags dropping, then laughter

Diana How's Gordon?
Marge Not too bad.

Marge bustles in laden with bags. Diana follows

Marge Poor little thing—lying there—with his face as white as a sheet . . .
Diana Poor thing . . .
Marge (*putting the bags on the sofa*) He looks dreadful . . . Hallo, Evelyn.
Evelyn Hallo.
Marge Oh! (*Going to the pram*) Look who's here! Little baby Walter.
Evelyn Wayne.
Marge What?
Evelyn It's Wayne. His name's Wayne.
Diana (*laughing*) Walter . . .
Marge I thought it was Walter.
Diana Marge, honestly. You can't have a baby called Walter.
Marge Well, I don't know. Somebody must have done . . . (*She screams with laughter. Peering into the pram*) Oh look. Look at his skin. It's a lovely skin, Evelyn.
Evelyn Thank you.
Marge Beautiful skin. Hallo, Baby Wayne. Hallo, Wayne. Google—google—google.
Diana Ssh, Marge, she's just got him to sleep.
Marge (*quieter*) Diggy diggy diggy. (*Whispering*) Lovely when they're asleep.
Diana Yes . . .
Marge (*whispering*) Looks like his daddy. Looks like John.
Diana You don't have to whisper, Marge. Just don't shout in his ear.

Marge (*going back to her carriers, etc.*) Look at all this lot. I can't go anywhere.
Diana What have you got there?
Marge You know what I'm like. You know me . . . Oh, guess what I did get? (*She puts the bags near the sofa*)
Diana What?
Marge Are you ready?
Diana Yes.
Marge Brace yourself. I got the shoes.
Diana You bought them?
Marge Just now and I don't care. I passed the shop on the way here. I thought it's no good, I don't care, it's now or never, I'm going to have them, I must have them. So I got them.
Diana I must see.
Marge Just a minute. Gordon'll go mad . . . (*Rummaging*) Now, which one did I put them in?
Diana It is a shame about Gordon. Gordon's ill, Evelyn, he can't come.
Evelyn Oh.
Marge No. He finally got it. It's been going round and round for months, I knew he'd get it eventually. He was perfectly all right last night, then he woke up this morning and he'd got it . . . (*Finding her shoe bag within another bag*) Here we are . . . (*Finding something else*) Oh—nearly forgot. That's for you.
Diana For me?
Marge It's only a little thing. But I saw one while I was in there and I knew you'd seen mine and wanted one . . .
Diana Oh, yes . . .
Marge (*to Evelyn*) It's a holder. For those paper towels in the kitchen. Paper-towel holder. Have you got one?
Evelyn No.
Marge Remind me, I'll get you one.
Diana That's so thoughtful (*Going for her handbag*) I must pay you for it.
Marge You'll do no such thing.
Diana No, Marge, I insist. You're always buying us things.
Marge I enjoy it. I like buying presents.
Diana (*producing her purse*) How much?

Evelyn rises and moves to the door to the stairs

Marge I won't take it, put it away.
Diana How much was it?
Marge Diana, will you put that purse away this minute.
Diana No, I'm sorry, Marge, I'm going to pay you.
Marge Diana, will you put that away this minute. Evelyn, tell her to put it away . . .
Diana (*to Evelyn*) You all right, dear?
Evelyn Fine.
Diana Where are you off to then?
Evelyn To the lavatory.
Diana Oh. I see. Beg your pardon.

Evelyn goes out upstairs

(*Selecting coins from her purse*) Twenty p. There you are. I don't know
how much it was but there you are.
Marge Oh, really. (*She leaves the money on the table*)
Diana Am I glad to see you!
Marge Why's that?
Diana She's been here for ages.
Marge Who do you mean—oh, yes. Miss Chatterbox.
Diana I know she's been up to something. I don't trust her. I never did.
Marge I must show you my shoes. (*She starts to unpack them*) How do
you mean?
Diana I know that girl's been up to something.
Marge Oh, you mean with . . . ?
Diana She and Paul. I know they have.
Marge Well . . . (*Producing a pair of very unsuitable shoes*) There, you see.
Aren't they nice?
Diana Lovely.
Marge They had them in blue which was nicer, actually. But then I had
nothing else that would have gone with them.
Diana He didn't want them to come round here today. That's how I
know they're up to something.
Marge Who? (*She tries on the shoes*)
Diana Evelyn and John. He didn't want them round.
Marge Who? Paul didn't?
Diana No.
Marge (*parading around in her shoes*) Look, you see—these tights aren't
right with them but . . .
Diana I mean, why should he suddenly not want them round? They've
been round here enough in the past and then all of a sudden he doesn't
want to see them.
Marge Odd. There was another sort, you know, with the strap but I
found they cut me across here.
Diana They suit you.
Marge Yes, I'm very pleased. (*She sits in the armchair*)
Diana I tried to get her to say something.
Marge Evelyn?
Diana Just now.
Marge Oh. Did she?
Diana No. She's not saying anything. Why should she? I know Paul, you
see. I know he's with someone. I'm sure it's her. He came home, went
straight upstairs and washed his shirt through the other night. I said,
what's got into you? He said, well what's wrong with me washing my
shirt? I said you've never washed anything in your life. He said, well,
we all have to start sometime. I said, lovely but why do you want to
start doing it in the middle of the night for. And he had no answer to
that at all. Nothing. He just stood there with it dripping all over the
floor.
Marge Well . . .

Diana After twelve years, you get to know someone.

Marge I wonder if these will go with that other coat.

Diana What's she doing up there?

Marge Well, she's . . .

Diana I bet she's having a really good snoop around.

Marge Oh, Di . . .

Diana I bet that's what she's up to. I've never trusted her an inch. She's got one of those really mean little faces, hasn't she?

Marge Well . . .

Diana I bet it was her that went off with my scarf, you know.

Marge I shouldn't think so. Why don't you talk it over with Paul?

Diana Paul? We haven't talked for years. Not really. Now he's had his own way and sent the children off to school, there's even less to talk about. I don't know why he wanted them at boarding school. They're neither of them happy. I know they're not. You should see the letters they write.

Marge I don't know what to say . . . (*Moving to the pram*) Poogy, poogy. Hallo, Walter.

Diana Wayne.

Marge Hallo.

Diana Don't for God's sake wake him up. He's been bawling his head off half the afternoon. I don't think she feeds him properly.

Marge He looks nice and chubby.

Diana It doesn't look all there to me.

Marge Di!

Diana No, truthfully, you look at its eyes.

Marge He's asleep.

Diana Well, you look at them when it wakes up. Don't tell me that's normal. I mean, our Mark's were never like that. Nor were Julie's. And she's had to wear glasses.

Marge She looks lovely in her little glasses.

Diana Paul doesn't think so. He won't let her wear them when she's at home.

Marge Well, I think he's a lovely baby. (*Returning to the armchair*) I was on at Gordon again the other day about adopting one.

Diana What did he say?

Marge Still no. He won't hear of it. He's frightened of it, I think. He keeps saying to me, it's not like a dog, Marge. We can't get rid of it if we don't like it and I say, we will like it, we'll grow to like it and then he says, well what happens if we adopt one and then it grows up to be a murderer? Then what do we do? They'll blame us.

Diana It's not very likely.

Marge Try convincing him. No, he's just going to keep on going with his tests—till the cows come home. That reminds me, I must ring him up. I said I would as soon as I got here. See if he's coping. Do you mind? (*She moves to the telephone*)

Diana No, go ahead.

Marge He's got the phone by his bed.

Marge dials

Evelyn enters from the stairs

Diana Find everything?
Evelyn Fine. (*She checks the baby with a glance then sits and starts to read a magazine*)
Diana Marge is just phoning her husband.
Evelyn Oh.
Marge (*as she stands waiting for an answer; indicating her shoes*) Do you like these, Evelyn?
Evelyn Fantastic.
Marge (*into the phone*) Hallo . . . Jumjums? It's Margie, darling. How are you feeling? . . . Oh—oh. Well listen, Jumjums, can you manage to get across to the chest of drawers, sweetie? . . . By the window, yes . . . You'll find them in the top drawer . . . That's right, darling . . . Can you manage that all right on your own? . . . Right (*Pause. To Diana*) He wants the nose drops, he's all bunged up, poor love . . . (*She stands listening*)
Diana (*to Evelyn*) What are you chewing, dear?
Evelyn Gum.
Diana Oh.
Evelyn Want a bit?
Diana No thanks. We'll be having our tea soon.
Marge (*into the phone*) Oh, darling—you must be careful, Jumjums . . . Yes, I know it shouldn't be there . . . Never mind, well rub it, rub it better. (*Covering the phone, to the others*) Banged his leg. (*Into the phone*) All right? I'll be here if you want me. You know the number. I'll be home soon . . . Yes . . . Yes, I will. I'll phone you later. Bye-bye, Jumjums, bye-bye, darling . . . Bye. (*Pause*) Bye-bye. (*Pause*) Bye. (*She rings off*) Honestly, I don't know what I want children for, living with Gordon. I get through first-aid tins like loaves of bread. (*She returns to the armchair*)
Diana He's very unlucky, isn't he?
Marge Oh, he is. He's so big, you see. I think that's one of his troubles. Being so big. Nothing's really made his size. He bangs his head on buses. He can't sit down in the cinema and he has trouble getting into his trousers. It's a terrible problem. Sixteen stone eight.
Diana Yes, that is big.
Marge It is, it's very big. His face is small but then he's got quite a small head. It's the rest of him. Somebody the other day said he looked like a polythene bag full of water. (*She laughs*)

Diana laughs

Oh, dear, you have to laugh.
Diana Poor Gordon. It's not fair.
Marge He's all right. Bless him. Keeps me out of mischief.

Diana and Marge laugh. A silence. They look at Evelyn, who chews on, reading

Diana (*with a look at Marge*) Enjoying that, are you?

Evelyn It's all right . . .
Marge Oh. I've still got these on. (*She goes to the sofa to change her shoes*)
Diana Be funny seeing Colin again. Three years.
Marge I only knew him slightly. He was Gordon's friend really.
Diana Yes. It's a pity he'll miss Colin.
Marge What exactly happened to this fiancée of his? Did she just die?
Diana Drowned.
Marge Drowned, oh . . .
Diana In the sea.
Marge Oh.

Throughout the following Marge follows Diana's lips carefully, echoing the odd word in agreement

Diana We knew him very well, you know. He and Paul were inseparable. And then Colin's job moved him away and he used to write to us occasionally and then he wrote and said he'd met this Carol girl and that they were going to get married—which was a great surprise to us because we always said he'd never let anything get that far and then the next thing we heard, she'd drowned. So I said to Paul, we'd better invite him over. I mean, we're still his friends. I doubt if he's got any where he is now because it takes him ages to get to know people and then I thought, well, it might be awkward, embarrassing knowing what to say to him, just Paul and me and since he knew Gordon and you slightly and John—he doesn't know Evelyn of course—I thought it would be nice if we just had a little tea party for him. He'll need his friends.
Marge Well, you know me, I'm bound to say the wrong thing so shut me up or I'll put my foot in it. Was she young?
Diana Who?
Marge His fiancée.
Diana Carol? About his age, I think.
Marge Oh. Tragic.
Diana Yes. (*Aware of Evelyn again*) What are you reading, dear?
Evelyn Nothing.
Diana No, what is it?
Evelyn (*wearily turning back a page and reading flatly*) "Your happiness is keeping that man in your life happy. Twelve tips by a woman psychiatrist."
Diana Oh.
Marge We can all learn from that.
Evelyn (*reading on remorselessly*) "Tip number one: send him off in the morning with a smile. How many of us first thing just don't bother to make that little extra effort. Have you ever graced the breakfast table without a comb through your hair. Go on, admit it, of course you have. You're only human. Or done that little extra something to take the shine off your early morning nose. No wonder he escapes behind his paper . . ."
Diana I must read that.
Evelyn (*unstoppable*) "Go on, live a little and give him the surprise of his life."

Diana Yes, that's lovely, Evelyn . . .

Evelyn "Make yourself into his news of the day. You'll live with him till the evening. Tip number two: go on, pamper yourself with a full beauty treatment."

Diana Yes, thank you, Evelyn.

Evelyn What?

Diana That's lovely. I'll read it later.

Marge We can all learn something from that.

Evelyn I'm not doing that for my bloody husband. He can stuff it.

Pause

Marge I'd hate to drown. (*Pause*) I don't mind anything else. Poison, hanging, shooting—that's never worried me but I'd hate to drown. You look so awful afterwards.

Diana Now, we mustn't get morbid. We're here to cheer Colin up when he comes. I know this all happened two months ago now but he's bound to be a bit down. We mustn't let him dwell on it.

Marge No. You're quite right.

A silence

> *Paul enters from outside. He has on his track-suit bottoms and a sweater. He has obviously been taking exercise*

Paul (*as he comes in*) Have you seen my shoes anywhere . . .? (*Breaking off as he sees that they have company*) Oh, hallo there.

Marge Hallo, Paul.

Evelyn (*barely glancing up*) 'Lo.

Paul Mothers' Meeting is it? How are you, Marge?

Marge Very well, thank you.

Paul How about you, Evelyn?

Evelyn Eh?

Paul Keeping fit?

Evelyn Yes.

Paul (*looking into the pram*) What's in here then? Tomorrow's dinner?

Evelyn No.

Paul Oh. I thought it was tomorrow's dinner.

Diana Did you have a good game?

Paul All right. So so. Not really. Dick didn't turn up. Had to play with this other fellow. Useless. Finished up giving him eight start and playing left-handed. I still beat him. Then he fell over his racquet and broke his glasses so we called it a day. Trouble with that club is, you couldn't improve your game even if you wanted to. No competition. Lot of flabby old men.

Evelyn (*without looking up*) Hark at Mr Universe.

Paul Watch it. (*To Diana*) You seen my black shoes?

Diana Which ones?

Paul The black ones.

Diana They're upstairs.

Paul Well, they weren't there this morning. How's Gordon?

Marge He's not too good today, I'm afraid.
Paul Not again.
Diana What do you mean, not again?
Paul He's always ill. Gordon.
Marge Not always.
Paul Hasn't been to work for two years, has he?
Marge 'Course he has.
Diana He's exaggerating.
Paul He's a one man casualty ward. Why don't you get him insured, Marge? You'd clean up in a couple of days.
Marge Get on . . .
Paul Right. I'll leave you ladies to it, if you don't mind. Ta ta. Look after yourselves. I've things to do upstairs.
Diana Don't be too long, will you, dear?
Paul How do you mean?
Diana I mean, don't stay up there for too long.
Paul No, I've just got a bit of work to do, that's all.
Diana Well, tea will be in a minute. You'll be down for that.
Paul No. You don't want me down here, I'll . . .
Diana You must come down for tea. Colin's coming.
Paul Colin who?
Diana Colin. You know, Col . .
Paul Oh, that Colin. Is he?
Diana Oh, don't be so stupid. You know he is. I told you.
Paul Did you?
Diana I arranged it a fortnight ago.
Paul You never told me.
Diana And I reminded you this morning.
Paul You didn't tell me.
Diana This morning, I told you.
Paul Excuse me, you did not tell me he was coming this morning. You did not tell me anything this morning. I was out before you were up.
Diana Well, then it must have been yesterday morning.
Paul That's more likely. But you still didn't tell me.
Diana I told you very distinctly.
Marge Perhaps you just forgot, Paul.
Paul No. I'm sorry I didn't forget. I never forget things. You're talking to the wrong man. I run a business where it's more than my life's worth to forget things. I've trained myself not to. I never forget.
Marge Well, I'm sorry I . . .
Paul Yes, all right. Just don't give me that "maybe you forgot bit" because with me it doesn't cut any ice at all . . .
Diana Look, Paul, will you stop taking it out on Marge for some reason . . .
Paul I'm not taking it out on anybody. Look, I've got a lot of work to do upstairs . . .
Diana Now, Paul, you can't do that. Colin is coming. He is your friend. You can't just go upstairs . . .
Paul Excuse me, he is not a friend of mine. He was never a friend of mine . . .

Diana How can you say that?
Paul I just happened to know him, that's all. You'll just have to say to him when he comes that you're sorry, I had no idea he was coming, nobody told me and that I had a lot of work to do upstairs.
Diana You cannot do that . . .
Paul I'm sorry . . .
Diana You've got no work to do.
Paul That's it. No more. I'm not going on with it. I'm going upstairs. I don't want to hear any more about it. I have a lot of work to do. Excuse me please.

Paul goes out upstairs

A silence

Diana I told him Colin was coming. I told him over breakfast. While he was eating his cereal. I told him. He always does this. Every time I . . . (*Tearfully*) I spent ages getting this ready.
Marge It's all right, Di . . .
Diana It's not all right. He's always doing this. He does it all the time. I told him. Specially . . .

Diana hurries out into the kitchen

Marge Oh dear.

Evelyn gives an amused grunt, ostensibly at her magazine. Marge looks at her. Evelyn sits in the armchair with her magazine. Marge takes knitting out of her bag and starts knitting on the sofa

Evelyn, could I have a word with you?
Evelyn What?
Marge I want you to answer me something perfectly honestly. I want you to be absolutely straight with me. Will you do that, please?
Evelyn What?
Marge It's been brought to my notice that you and Paul—have—well . . .
Evelyn What?
Marge I think you know what I'm talking about.
Evelyn No.
Marge That you and her husband have been—is this true? Yes or no?
Evelyn Is what true?
Marge Will you put that magazine down a moment, please.
Evelyn (*laying the magazine aside wearily*) Well?
Marge Is it true or isn't it? Yes or no?
Evelyn What?
Marge Have you been—having—a love affair with Paul?
Evelyn No.
Marge Truthfully?
Evelyn I said no.
Marge Oh. Well. That's all right then.

Pause

Evelyn We did it in the back of his car the other afternoon but I wouldn't call that a love affair.
Marge You and Paul did?
Evelyn Yes.
Marge How disgusting.
Evelyn It wasn't very nice.
Marge And you have the nerve to come and sit in her house . . .
Evelyn She asked me. (*Pause*) She needn't worry. I'm not likely to do it again. He'd just been playing squash, he was horrible.
Marge Diana knows about this, you know.
Evelyn Then he must have told her. I didn't.
Marge She's not a fool. She put two and two together. He didn't want you to come here at all this afternoon. That's a sure sign of a guilty conscience.
Evelyn Most probably because he doesn't like me very much.
Marge He liked you enough to . . .
Evelyn Not after what I said to him.
Marge What did you say?
Evelyn I said thank you very much. That was as exciting as being made love to by a sack of clammy cement and would he kindly drive me home.
Marge That wasn't a very nice thing to say.
Evelyn He's horrible.
Marge What a thing to say.
Evelyn Horrible. Worse than my husband and that's saying a lot.
Marge Poor John. God help him being married to you.
Evelyn Why?
Marge Well. Really.
Evelyn They all think they're experts with women. None of them are usually. And by the time they are, most of them aren't up to it any more.
Marge You speak for yourself.
Evelyn I am. I've tried enough of them to know. (*She reads*)
Marge Your husband will catch up with you one of these days.
Evelyn He knows.
Marge He knows!
Evelyn Nothing he can do.
Marge Does he know about you and Paul?
Evelyn Probably. He's not going to complain.
Marge Why not?
Evelyn Well—he relies on Paul for business, doesn't he? Without Paul, he's in trouble. Business before pleasure that's John's motto.
Marge Sounds as if it's yours as well.
Evelyn There's not much pleasure to be had round this place, is there?
Marge I'm sorry, I find your attitude quite disgusting. Heartless, cruel and disgusting. (*She stands and goes to the pram*)

Evelyn ignores her and continues her reading

(*At the pram*) Poor little child. If only he knew. Poor little Walter. Googy, googy . . . You're just a heartless little tart—googy, googy.

Evelyn If you're interested, those shoes of yours are a lousy buy.
Marge And what would you know about my shoes?
Evelyn I bought a pair. They split at the sides after two days and the dye comes off on your feet.
Marge I've nothing further to say to you.
Evelyn Anyway, they're out of fashion.
Marge I don't wish to listen to you any further.

The doorbell rings. They both wait

One of us had better answer that, hadn't we?
Evelyn Yes.

The doorbell rings

Marge I suppose it had better be me.

Diana enters

Diana That was the doorbell, wasn't it?
Marge Oh, was it? Yes, we thought we heard it.
Diana What if it's Colin? I don't know what I'm going to say if it is . . .

Diana goes out to the front door

Marge You see what you've done.
Evelyn Beg your pardon?
Marge (*sitting on the sofa*) To them. To Paul and her. See the atmosphere between them. All your doing.
Evelyn Me?
Marge Who else?
Evelyn You really want to know who else?
Marge I hope you realize that.
Evelyn If you really want to know who else, you'd better pass me the phone book. He's half-way through the Yellow Pages by now. If it moves, he's on to it.

John enters—a jiggling, restless figure. Diana follows, then exits upstairs

John Hallo, hallo.
Marge Hallo, John.
Evelyn You took your time.
John It's only twenty past.
Evelyn You took your time.
John (*amiably*) Yes. (*He jigs about*)
Marge Where's Di gone to?
John Dunno. Upstairs, I think. (*Sticking his head into the pram*) Hallo, son. Say hallo to daddy.
Evelyn Don't.
John Eh?
Evelyn He's asleep.
John He shouldn't be. He won't sleep tonight now.

Evelyn He never does anyway.

John Keep him awake during the day, that's the secret. Shake his rattle in his ear every ten minutes.

Evelyn Fantastic.

John Where's Paul?

Marge Upstairs.

John Oh. Both gone to bed have they? (*He laughs*)

Marge glares at Evelyn

No Colin yet?

Marge Not yet.

John Well, I hope he hurries it up. Then we can get it over with.

Evelyn I thought he was supposed to be a friend of yours.

John He was, yes.

Evelyn Sounds like it.

John I haven't seen him for years. Anyway—I don't know what to say to him. I didn't know this girl of his. I mean, it's difficult.

Marge I don't think he'll want to talk about Carol.

John No?

Marge I shouldn't think so. He'll want to forget.

John I hope so. I hate death. Gives me the creeps.

Evelyn Get on.

John It does.

Evelyn You?

John I get all—uggghhh. (*He shudders*) Don't talk about it.

Evelyn (*laughing*) Death, death, death.

John Shut up.

Evelyn laughs. Silence. Marge takes up her knitting

Marge I hope they come down before he arrives.

John Disgraceful. On a Saturday afternoon. Whatever next. (*Pause. He jigs about some more*) I got that fuel gauge.

Evelyn Oh.

John Ninety p. off it. (*He laughs*) It had a loose wire. I told the girl it was faulty. She didn't know any better. Ninety p. (*Pause*) Got a wing mirror for thirty p. Had a screw missing off it. Got one of those round the corner and he let me have some interior carpet for nothing. He was throwing it away. Not a bad day's work, eh?

Evelyn Great.

John You're the one who wanted carpet in the car.

Evelyn Fine.

John Can't do anything right, can I?

Evelyn I just know you. It won't fit when you get it in.

John It'll fit.

Evelyn No, it won't because you got it cheap.

John It'll fit.

Evelyn Nothing you ever get for us is quite right. I've got a vacuum cleaner with elastic bands holding on the attachments because you got them cheap off another model.

John Oh, come on.

Evelyn I've got an electric mixer I can't use because it flings the food half-way up the bloody wall.

John It's only because it's got the wrong bowl that's all. Only the bowl's wrong.

Evelyn Then why haven't we got the right bowl?

John I'm trying to get hold of one. They're scarce.

Evelyn But it never did have the right bowl.

John I know it didn't. How do you think I got it cheap in the first place?

Evelyn Oh, I give up. (*She reads*)

John You're just a trouble maker you are. (*He playfully shadow-boxes near her face*) Bam, bam . . .

Evelyn Go away.

John shadow-boxes round the room

Diana enters

John Here she is. Had a good time up there?

Marge Is Paul coming down?

Diana I have no idea. I have no idea at all. I have done my best. I have now given up. Most probably it will be left to us. In which case, we'll have to cope with Colin on our own, won't we?

John Without Paul?

Diana Apparently he's far too busy to see his so-called best friend. (*She sits on the sofa*)

John If Paul's not going to be here, it's going to be a bit . . .

Diana Quite. What's that you're knitting, Marge?

Marge Oh, just a sweater for Gordon.

Diana Lovely colour.

Marge Yes, I rather like it. I'm hoping he'll wear it to protect his chest. Once he goes out in that wind . . .

John How is old Gordon? Is he coming?

Marge I'm afraid he's not very well at the moment.

John Oh, dear. He's had this a long time, hasn't he?

Marge Had what?

John This—er food poisoning, wasn't it?

Marge That was weeks ago. This is something quite different.

John Oh. (*He jigs about*)

Diana Would you like to take a seat, John?

John No, it's all right, thanks. I don't like sitting down very much.

Evelyn Sit down, for heaven's sake.

John I don't like sitting down. I don't enjoy it.

Evelyn He'll never sit down. I don't think I've ever seen him sit down. He has his meals dancing around the table.

John I prefer standing up, that's all.

Pause. John jiggles violently

Diana (*tense and shrill*) John, will you please sit down before you drive me mad.

John (*sitting*) Sorry. Sorry . . . (*He sits on the hearth bench*)
Diana I'm sorry.
John No, it's me, I'm sorry.
Diana I'm sorry, John.
John No need to be sorry. That's all right.
Evelyn You'll never get him to sit still, I'll tell you that.

Evelyn sits, chews and reads. John tries not to fidget, then picks up the towel-holder from the bag and beats time with it. Diana looks at him sharply. He mouths "sorry" and puts it down. Diana sits staring ahead of her, steeped in worry. Marge studies her pattern

Marge (*at length*) I think I've gone wrong with this. I've got twelve too many stitches. How the dickens did I get twelve too many stitches?

At length Paul enters from the stairs

John (*jumping up*) Hallo, hallo, he's arrived. (*He puts down the towel-holder*)

Paul stands, surveying the room, making his presence felt, then sits on the bench John has vacated

Paul Well. Here I am then.
Diana So we see.
Paul That's what you wanted, wasn't it?
Diana I'm not so sure.
Paul Well, make up your mind. I'll go upstairs again.

Silence

John Paul, could we have a quick word about Eastfield, do you think?
Paul Not just at the moment, if you don't mind.
John It's just if I got your okay, I could go ahead with the order.
Paul Look, I'm not in the mood to talk about Eastfield just at the moment, John. We're having this riotous tea party. Rude to talk business over tea. (*He discovers the paper towel-holder*) What's this? Where did this come from?
Diana It's nothing. It's just a holder for the paper towel in the kitchen, that's all.
Paul Is it ours?
Diana Yes.
Paul What have you gone and bought another one for?
Diana I didn't.
Paul I just put one up the other day. How many of the things do you want?
Marge Oh well . . .
Paul (*laughing to Marge*) Kitchen, knee-deep in paper towels.
Marge It's useful to have a spare.

Pause

Paul I don't know what we're going to talk to this fellow about, I'm sure. We haven't seen him for three years. I don't even know this girl's name.
Diana Carol.

Paul Well, that's something. I mean, I can't see what good this is going to do for him. Coming round here talking to us about it.
Diana He probably won't want to.
Paul Then what else is there to talk about? It's just embarrassing isn't it?
Diana What's embarrassing? Somebody you've known for a long time loses someone very dear to them. Seems natural to ask them round and comfort them a little.
Paul Fat lot of comfort he'll get here.
Marge We can try. It'll only be for an hour.
John As long as he doesn't start talking about death, I don't mind. If he starts on about death or dying, I'm off.
Evelyn I don't know why you came.
John Well—like Di says, it's—friendly.
Evelyn You don't like him.
John Colin? I didn't mind him.
Evelyn You said you didn't like him.
John I didn't mind him.
Paul I didn't like him.
Diana You went round with him enough.
Paul I did not.
Diana You used to come round to our house every Friday and Saturday. You and him. We used to call you the flower-pot men.
Paul He used to follow me.
Diana And Colin always went off with my sister Barbara and I was stuck with you.

John and Marge laugh

Paul Very funny.
Diana It's true. We both fancied Colin really.

John and Marge laugh again

Paul That is patently untrue. That is a lie.
Diana I was only joking . . .
Paul If you want to know what it really was . . .
Diana I was joking.
Paul (*rising*) If you really want to know . . .
Diana It was a joke.

Paul subsides and sits again

Paul Anyway. Come to that, why do you think we both came round?
Diana I don't doubt it.
Paul Well.
Diana You lost out then, didn't you?
Paul So did you.
Diana You said it, not me.
Marge Look, we really mustn't quarrel.
Diana I'm not quarrelling.
Paul Neither am I.
Marge I mean, Colin's not going to want this. He'll want to feel he's among friends, not enemies.

Evelyn (*in her magazine*) This is a rotten story in here. This fellow's gone mad just because this girl's kissed him. Running about and singing.
Marge I think that's meant to be romantic, Evelyn.
Evelyn They ought to put him away for good, if you ask me.
Diana If you really fancied Barbara, I'm surprised you didn't go off with her. You had the chance.
Paul Forget I said it.
Diana I mean, why didn't you?
Paul Would you all please witness I did not start this conversation?
Diana Answer me that.
Paul You are all witnesses, thank you.
Diana If you fancied her that much . . .
Paul Oh, God.
Diana Never mind. You're making up for it now, aren't you?
Paul What do you mean by that?
Marge Now, Di . . .
Diana I said, you're making up for it now, aren't you, dearest? With your other little . . .
Marge Why don't we all have a cup of tea now? Wouldn't that be a nice idea?

The phone starts ringing

Paul No. I want that last remark explained if you don't mind.
Marge (*rising*) Now, Paul, Paul . . .
Diana Never mind.
Paul (*rising*) All my other what?
Marge (*standing between them, arms outstretched*) Now, Di—Paul . . .
Diana You know.
John Should I answer that?
Paul All my other what? I want to hear the rest of that sentence.
Diana You know perfectly well what I'm talking about.
Marge Di—Paul . . .
John I'll answer it, shall I? (*He goes to the phone*)
Paul I have not the slightest idea what you're talking about, I'm sorry.
Diana (*pointing at Evelyn*) Well, I'm sure she has. Ask her then.
Marge Di—Paul . . .
Evelyn Eh?
John (*into the phone*) Hallo . . . Could you speak up please.
Diana Yes, you. Don't you sit there looking so innocent and smug. I know all about you.
Paul What are you dragging Evelyn into this for?
John (*into the phone*) Oh, hallo Gordon. (*To Marge*) It's Gordon.
Marge Gordon. Oh, my God. (*She snatches the phone from John*)
Diana If anyone has dragged Evelyn into this, it's you.
Marge (*into the phone*) Hallo, Jumjums.
Diana You're the one who's dragged her in, literally.
Marge (*into the phone*) My darling, what is it?
Paul I don't know what you're talking about. Will somebody kindly tell me what she's talking about.

Marge (*to the others*) He's spilt his cough mixture in his bed.

Diana You know bloody well what I'm talking about. I'm talking about you and her, you bastard.

Marge (*into the phone*) Has it sunk through to the mattress, love?

Evelyn I'm going home.

Diana Yes, you go home, you little bitch.

Paul Oh, no you don't. You stay where you are, Evelyn. If she says things like that, she's got to prove them.

Diana I don't have to. I know.

Evelyn Good-bye. (*She pushes the pram towards the front door*)

John We can't go now. Colin's coming. (*He goes to the pram*)

Evelyn To hell with him. (*She turns back to collect her handbag*)

Paul She's just hysterical.

Marge Can you try and sleep on the dry side until I get back?

Paul The woman's hysterical. Now listen, Di . . . (*He tries to sit next to Diana*)

Diana (*screaming*) Don't come near me.

Marge (*into the phone*) Oh no. Have you got it on your 'jamas as well?

The baby starts crying

Evelyn (*furiously*) You've woken him up now. (*She goes to the pram*)

John I didn't wake him up.

Paul I mean, seriously, how can a man live with a woman like that?

Marge (*into the phone*) Jumjums, how did you get it on your trousers . . . Well, look, take them off, dear. Take the bottoms off.

John Where are you going?

Evelyn (*starting to push the pram out*) I'm taking him home.

John Oh, Evelyn . . .

Evelyn exits

Paul I mean, am I unreasonable?

Marge (*into the phone*) There's some more in the bottom drawer. The stripy ones.

John (*calling after her*) Evelyn.

Marge (*into the phone*) Yes, well, you will be sticky. You'll have to wash

The doorbell rings

Diana How you can stand there looking so damned innocent . . .

Paul Listen, if you could tell me what I'm being accused of, I could perhaps answer you.

The doorbell rings

John I think that's the doorbell.

Marge (*into the phone*) Now, keep warm, Jumjums, keep warm . . .

Evelyn re-enters with the pram, the baby still crying

John What are you doing?

Evelyn I can't get out that way. There's somebody at the front door.
Diana Get out of my house.
Evelyn I'm trying to.
Marge (*into the phone*) Bye-bye, darling.
John It'll be Colin.
Marge (*into the phone*) Bye.
Paul Colin?
Evelyn I'm taking Wayne in the garden.
Marge (*into the phone*) Bye. (*She hangs up*)
John Don't go home, Evelyn.
Paul Now listen, Di, Marge . . .
Evelyn (*as she goes out*) I can't, can I?

Evelyn goes out to the garden with the pram. John follows

Marge He has spilt cough mixture not only on the sheet, but on the pillow.

The doorbell rings

Paul Would you listen a minute?
Marge —his clean pyjama bottoms . . .
Paul Marge, please. Would you mind? Di, get a grip on yourself, Di.
Diana What?
Paul Colin is here now at the door.
Diana Oh no.

Diana runs out to the kitchen

Paul Di . . .
Marge Shall I let him in?
Paul Would you mind, Marge. You seem to be the calmest among us.
Marge I am not calm, believe me. That linctus will have gone through that undersheet straight into that mattress. (*As she goes*) I don't know how I'm going to get it out, I don't.

Marge exits to the front door. John enters from the garden

Paul paces. John jiggles

Paul Did you tell her?
John Who?
Paul Di.
John What about?
Paul About Evelyn and me.
John I didn't. Why should I? I mean, as we said, it was just one of those things, wasn't it?
Paul Right.
John Wouldn't happen again.
Paul Certainly wouldn't.
John There you are. We'd settled it, hadn't we?

Paul Did Evelyn tell Di?
John I don't think so.
Paul Can't see why she would.
John No reason at all. Just one of those things, wasn't it? I'm not bitter.
It was a bit of a shock when she told me. But I'm not bitter.
Paul Somebody told her . . .

Marge ushers in Colin

Marge Here he is.
Colin Paul.
Paul Colin, my old mate, how are you? (*He embraces Colin*)
Colin Great to see you. John . . .
John (*shaking his hand*) Hallo, Col.
Colin Oh, it is good to see you both. How are you?
Paul Great.
John Fine.
Colin Where are the girls then, where are the girls?
Paul Oh—er—Di's just out in the kitchen there.
Colin Doing her stuff?
Paul Yes, more or less. And—er—Evelyn's with the baby.
Colin Hey, yes. You've got a baby.
John Right.
Colin Boy or girl?
John Boy. Wayne. Four months.
Colin Fantastic. That's what you always wanted, didn't you? I always
remember that. When the four of us used to get together, you know,
you, me, Gordon, Paul—what was it Gordon wanted to be, a cricketer,
wasn't it?—you always used to say, I just want to get married and have
a son.
John Right.
Colin Fantastic. Congratulations. Sorry to hear about Gordon, Marge.
He's ill, you say?
Marge I'm afraid so.
Colin Poor Gordon, he has all the luck. He wasn't feeling too good when
I left, was he? That's right. He was sick at the farewell party.
Marge Something he ate.
Colin (*to the others, laughing*) Out of me way, out of me way. Do you
remember. We were all sitting there, quietly talking and then, out of me
way, out of me way. Rushing about the room, everybody scattering for
cover. He flings open the door and throws up in the broom cupboard.
(*He laughs*) Nothing serious, I hope?
Marge No, no. He always looks worse than he is. (*With a laugh*) I don't
think he's quite at death's door yet.

Pause

Colin Good.
Marge I'll—see you in a minute.
Colin Right.

Marge goes to the kitchen

This is all right, this place, isn't it? Very nice indeed. How long have
you had this, Paul?
Paul Oh, nearly two years.
Colin Now we know where the money's going. I'd settle for this. Wouldn't
you, John? Yes, I'd settle for this.
John Yes.
Paul You want to sit down?
Colin Thanks. (*He sits in the armchair*) Very nice.
Paul (*sitting on the downstage bar-stool*) How are you feeling?

John sits on the sofa arm

Colin Oh, pretty fair. Lost a bit of weight lately, that helps. .
John Yes. (*He stands*)
Paul (*offering a cigar*) Col?
Colin No thanks.

Paul takes a cigar, then as an afterthought throws one to John, who catches it

John Thanks, Paul.
Colin What's your wife's name again, John, I forget? Before I meet her.
John Evelyn. (*He clicks his lighter intermittently in an effort to make it
work*)
Colin Evelyn. That's it. Di did write and tell me. I forgot. Sorry.
John That's okay. I forget it myself sometimes.

Colin laughs

Colin She's not local though, is she?
John No. She's got relatives.
Colin Ah. Will I approve, do you think?
John Eh?
Colin Do you think I'll approve of her?
John Well, yes. Hope so.
Colin She all right, is she, Paul?
Paul Eh?
Colin This Evelyn of his? Has he done all right for himself would you say?
Paul Oh, yes he's done all right.
Colin John could always pick them.
Paul Yes.

*Pause. John goes to the bar, lights his cigar with the lighter on it, then sits on
the sofa arm*

Marge enters with mats for the teapot and hot water jug

Marge (*whispering with embarrassment*) Excuse me. We're just brewing
up. Now, Di wants her handbag a minute. Is it . . .? Oh yes. Won't be
a minute.

Marge exits with Diana's handbag

Colin She hasn't changed.
Paul No.
Colin We used to have a name for her, didn't we? When Gordon first took her out.
Paul Can't remember.
Colin It was—can you, John?
John No. Something. I can't remember.
Paul No.
Colin It was a beetle or a spider or something. I'll remember, it'll come to me.

Pause

John You're looking well, Col.
Colin I feel well.
John You look it.

Pause

Colin I'm not early, am I?
Paul No, no . . .
John No.

Pause

Colin Yes. You've certainly done all right for yourself, haven't you, Paul?
Paul Now and again.
John Everything he touches.
Colin I bet. You two still fairly thick, I take it?
John Oh well, you know. When our paths cross. We do each other the odd favour.
Paul Generally one way.
John Oh, come on.
Paul Usually.
John Yes, usually. Not always, but usually.
Paul He's still the worst bloody salesman in the country. I'm the only one who'll buy his rotten stuff. I've got about five hundred tins of his rubbish. I can't give it away.
Colin What is it?
Paul Cat food. So called. That's what they call it. I've never met a cat yet who could eat it and live. Rubbish. I wouldn't give it to a dog.
Colin You could try it on Gordon.
John (*rising*) No, seriously for a moment, Paul, that's what I wanted to talk to you about. That particular line of ours isn't selling so well. It's not so much content, it's packaging. Now, they have just brought out this new line . . .
Paul Go on. They've discovered the antidote.

Colin laughs

John No, seriously, Paul.
Paul Not now.
John No, seriously, one word . . .

Paul Seriously, John, no.
John (*sitting again*) He'll be sorry.

Marge enters

Marge (*in the same embarrassed whisper, as before*) Excuse me a minute.
Just want to fetch my comb. For Di. Now where did I . . .? Oh yes.
*Marge finds her own handbag and bends and rummages in it. The men watch
her*
Colin The stick insect.
Marge (*startled*) What? (*She stands "angularly"*)
Colin Nothing.
The men laugh
Marge (*puzzled, waving the comb*) We won't be a minute. This is for Di.
A comb. For her hair. Excuse me.

Marge goes out

Paul Still at the bank, Colin?
Colin Yes. Still at the bank.
Paul That's what I like to hear.
Colin Yes.
Pause
Paul (*rising*) Look, I think I'll just go and see if I can sort them out out
there. Give them a hand. Excuse me.
Colin Of course.
Paul Won't be a sec.
Colin Right.

Paul goes out to the kitchen

*John and Colin rise. They sit. They rise, and meet in front of the table. They
laugh. They sit again—Colin in the armchair, John on the pouffe. They rise.
Colin looks at the picture behind the bar*

Great!
John Terrific!

Colin looks at a toy on the bar

John exits to the kitchen

Colin turns, sees he is alone, and sits back in his chair

*Diana enters with her handbag, Paul with the teapot followed by John,
Marge with the hot water jug. Evelyn enters from the garden*

Diana Hallo, Colin, I'm so sorry.

Colin Hallo, Di.

Diana and Colin kiss

Paul Back again.

John (*following Paul round and under the dialogue that follows*) No, the point I'm saying is, that if I were to knock off five per cent and sell the stuff to him for that much less, we could still net a profit of not less than what?—five twenties are a hundred—five eights are forty—less what?—three fives are fifteen—a hundred and twenty-five per cent. That's on an initial outlay—including transport of what?—four nines are thirty-six —plus, say, twenty for handling either end—that's fifty-six. Bring it to a round figure—sixty . . .

Paul, throughout this, nods uninterested agreement, his mind on other things. Over the above—

Diana It was so nice you could come. It really was. Now you know Marge, of course, don't you?

Colin Yes, yes.

Diana Oh, but you won't know Evelyn. This is John's Evelyn.

Colin How do you do.

Evelyn (*to Colin*) 'Lo.

Colin Heard a lot about you.

Evelyn Oh yes? Who from? (*She sits on the downstage bar-stool*)

Paul sits on the sofa

Colin Er . . .

Diana Sit down, Colin. Let me give you some tea. Sit down, everyone. (*To John, who is grinding on to Paul*) John dear, do sit down. (*She goes to the dining-table, puts her bag on it, brings down a dining-chair and puts it above the coffee table*)

John Oh yes, sorry. (*He sits on the pouffe*)

Marge moves to the pouffe. John rises and moves away. Diana sits on the chair and starts pouring tea. Marge sits on the pouffe

Colin Do you work at all, Evelyn, or does the baby take up all your time?

Evelyn No.

Colin Ah.

John She works some days.

Colin Oh yes, where's that?

Evelyn Part-time cashier at the Rollarena.

Colin Oh. Is that interesting?

Evelyn No.

Colin Ah.

Diana Could you pass these round, Paul? I remembered you liked it strong, Colin.

Paul passes round the various cups of tea

Colin Oh, lovely.

Pause. Diana passes the sugar to Colin

Marge Oh! Guess who I saw in the High Street?
Diana Who?
Marge Mrs Dyson. Grace Dyson.
Diana Oh, her.
Marge I was surprised. She looked well.

Paul sits on the sofa

Diana Good.

John moves to the bar

Paul Who's Grace Dyson?
Marge Oh well, you'd know her as Grace Follett probably.
Paul I don't think I know her at all.

Colin offers Evelyn sugar. John takes it

John Remember Ted Walker, Colin?
Colin Ted Walker? Oh, Ted Walker, yes. Of course, yes.
John He's still about.
Diana You like yours fairly weak, don't you, Marge?
Marge Yes, please. But don't drown it.

A silence. Diana moves to the sofa. John sits on the dining-chair

Colin Do you know what my biggest regret is?
Diana What's that, Colin?
Colin That none of you ever met Carol.
Marge Who?
Colin Carol. My ex-fiancée. She was drowned, you know.

John rises

Marge Oh, yes, yes. I know, I know.
Colin I wish you'd met her.
Diana Yes. (*Pause*) I think I can speak for all of us—(*she rises, then sits*)
—Colin, when I say how very sorry we were to hear about your loss.
As I hope you'll realize, we're your friends and—well—and although
we didn't know Carol—none of us had the pleasure of meeting her—
we feel that in a small way, your grief is our grief. After all, in this
world, we are all to some extent—we're all—what's the word . . . ?
Paul Joined.
Diana No.
John Related.
Marge Combined.
Diana No. Dependent.
Paul That's what I said.
Diana No you didn't, you said joined or something.
Paul It's the same thing. Joined, dependent, means the same.
Diana We are all dependent in a way for our own—and, well—no, I'm
sorry I've forgotten what I was going to say now. I hope you understand
what I meant, anyway.

Colin Thank you.

Diana (*embarrassed and relieved*) Oh well, that's got that over with, anyway. I mean—more tea, anyone?

Marge Give us a chance.

John sits back on the dining-chair. A silence. Colin suddenly slaps his knee and springs to his feet. Everyone jolts

What's the matter?

Colin Wait there, wait there.

Colin rushes out to the front door

Diana (*in a shocked whisper*) Where's he gone?

Paul I don't know.

Marge Is he all right?

Diana I didn't upset him, did I, saying that?

Marge No. Lovely.

John I'll have a look, shall I?

John exits to the front door

Diana Would you, John.

Paul What did you want to get on to that for?

Diana What?

Paul All that going on about grief and so on.

Diana I only said . . .

Paul (*rising*) We're supposed to be cheering him up. He didn't want to listen to that.

Diana It had to be said.

Marge You have to say it.

Paul (*moving above the sofa to the armchair*) He obviously didn't want to be reminded of it, did he? There was no need to, no need at all. We were all getting along perfectly happily.

Diana You can't sit here and not say anything about it.

John returns

John He's gone out the front door.

Diana Where to?

John His car, I think. He's getting something out of the boot.

Paul Probably going to hang himself with his tow rope. After what she said.

Diana He seemed perfectly recovered. Very cheerful. I thought someone should say something.

Paul Cheerful? You can see that was only skin deep.

Diana I couldn't.

Paul I was talking to him in here. You could tell. He's living on his nerves. On a knife edge. You could tell, couldn't you, John?

John He seemed quite cheerful.

Paul He could snap like that. Any minute. Same with anyone in this situation. Up one minute . . .
John I've never seen him quite so cheerful.

John exits to the front door

Paul Exactly. All the signs are there. The last thing he wanted to do was to talk about this fiancée of his. It's a known fact, people never . . .
Marge Oh yes, they do. My Aunt Angela . . .
Paul It is a known fact . . .

Slight pause. The front door bangs

John returns

John He's coming back.
Paul (*sitting in the armchair*) Now, not another word about her. Keep it cheerful. For God's sake, Evelyn, try and smile, just for once.

Colin enters. He carries a photo album and an envelope of loose snapshots, all contained at present, in a large chocolate box

All Ah . . .
Colin (*breathlessly*) Sorry. I forgot to bring these in. It's some photos. You can see what she looked like.
Diana Of her?
Colin Yes. I thought you'd like to.
Marge Oh.
Colin Yes. There's one or two quite good ones. Thought you might like to see some. Of course, if you'd rather . . .
Paul No, no . . .
Colin She was very photogenic. Shall I sit here next to you, Di? Then I can . . . (*He sits next to Diana*) Now then. (*Taking the snaps from the envelope*) Ah yes, these are some loose ones I haven't stuck in yet. They're the most recent. Can I give those to you, Marge? I think they're mostly on holiday, those. (*He hands the loose snapshots to Marge*)
Marge Thank you.
Colin (*with the album*) These are mostly at home in the garden at her house. (*He begins to open it*)
Marge Oh, is this her? Oh, she is lovely, Colin. Wasn't she?
Diana (*as Colin opens the first page*) Oh.
Colin There she is again. That's with her mum.
Diana She's a fine looking woman, too.
Colin Wonderful. She's been really wonderful. She's got this terrible leg.
Diana Ah.
Marge Oh, that's a nice one. Do you want to pass them round, John?
John Oh yes, sure.

Marge passes them to John who in due course passes them to Paul who passes them to Evelyn

Diana That's nice. Was that her house?
Colin No. That's the back of the Natural History Museum, I think.
Diana I was going to say . . .
Colin Went there at Easter.
Marge (*at a photo*) Oh.
Paul (*at a photo*) Ah.
Diana (*at the album*) Oh.
Marge Oh look, John, with her little dog, see?
John Oh yes.
Colin That was her mother's.
Marge Oh. Sweet little dog.
Evelyn I like that handbag.
Colin That's her again. Bit of a saucy one. It's not very good though, the sun's the wrong way.
Diana I wish I had a figure like that. It's so nice you brought them, Colin.
Marge Oh yes.
Diana It's nice, too, that you can look at them without—you know . . .
Colin Oh no, it doesn't upset me. Not now.
Marge That's wonderful.
Colin I was upset at the time, you know.
Diana Naturally.

John returns the photos to the table, then jiggles about

Colin But—after that—well, it's a funny thing about somebody dying—you never know, till it actually happens, how it's going to affect you. I mean, we all think about death at some time, I suppose, all of us. Either our death, somebody else's death. After all, it's one of the few things we have all got in common.
Diana Sit down, John.

John sits reluctantly on the hearth bench

Colin (*rising and collecting up the photos*) And I suppose when I first met Carol, it must have passed through my mind, what would I feel like if I did lose her. And I just couldn't think. I couldn't imagine it. I couldn't imagine my life going on without her. And then it happened. All of a sudden. One afternoon. All over. She was caught in this undercurrent, there was nothing anybody could do. I wasn't even around. They came and told me. And for about three weeks after that, I couldn't do anything at all. Nothing. I just lay about thinking, remembering and then, all of a sudden, it came to me that if my life ended there and then, by God, I'd have a lot to be grateful for. I mean, first of all, I'd been lucky enough to have known her. I don't know if you've ever met a perfect person. But that's what she was. The only way to describe her. And I, me, I'd had the love of a perfect person. And that's something I can always be grateful for. Even if for nothing else. And then I thought, what the hell am I talking about, my whole life's been like that. All through my childhood, the time I was growing up, all the time I lived here, I've had what a lot of people would probably give their right arm for—friends. Real friends, like John and Paul and Gordon and Di. So,

one of the things I just wanted to say, Di—Paul—Marge—John—
Evelyn and to Gordon if he was here, is that I'm not bitter about what
happened. Because I've been denied my own happiness, I don't envy or
begrudge you yours. I just want you to know that, despite everything
that happened, in a funny sort of way, I too am very happy.

*Colin smiles round at them serenely. A silence. A strange whooping noise. It
is Diana starting to weep hysterically. Unable to contain herself, she rushes
out. After a moment, Marge fumbles for her handkerchief and blows her
nose loudly. John, looking sickly, gives Colin a ghastly smile. Paul opens his
mouth as if to say something, gives up. Colin stands looking slightly bemused.
He looks at Evelyn. She looks back at him, expressionless, chewing*

Did I say the wrong thing?

Evelyn shrugs and resumes her reading, as—

the CURTAIN *falls*

ACT II

The same. Four-fifteen p.m.

The action is continuous. Everyone is there, except Diana

Colin (*worriedly*) I didn't say anything wrong, did I?
Paul No, no . . .
John I think she went to get the . . . (*He can't think of anything*)
Marge You know Di, Colin, she . . .
Colin Yes. Sorry.
Paul No, no . . .
Colin I'll pack these up. I didn't realize . . .
Marge No, no . . .
Colin Yes. It can be upsetting. I didn't realize . . .

Colin starts to gather up the rest of the photos. The others help by passing them to him

I bet I know what the trouble is, Paul.
Paul What?
Colin (*sitting on the sofa*) Di's been overdoing it again, hasn't she? That was always her trouble. She flings herself in to whatever she does. Heart and soul. Remember her with that jumble sale? I've still got this picture of her. Standing there, in the middle of all these old clothes, crying her heart out. Remember that?
Paul Yes.
Colin I mean, look at this tea. Whoever saw a tea like that.
John Any chance of a sandwich?
Marge (*rising*) Yes, I suppose we'd better . . . (*Holding up a plate of sandwiches*) John, would you like to pass these round, dear? Here, we've got some plates.

John rises and takes the sandwiches

Paul (*also rising*) It's all right, I'll . . .
Colin (*who has gathered in all his photos*) Is that the lot?
Marge (*handing Paul sideplates with paper napkins*) Here you are. (*To Colin*) We'd all love to have another look at them later.

Paul distributes plates and napkins

John (*passing round the sandwiches, muttering*) Great. (*After passing the sandwiches he retains the plate*)
Colin Yes, well, possibly. I hope Di's all right.
Paul Oh, yes . . .
Marge Oh, yes. She'll be fine. Fine. She's very sensitive.

Colin Oh, yes. I think that's what makes her a wonderful person, you know.

Marge Yes, yes. I think we could all learn from her example. She's so loyal and trusting . . . (*She sits in the dining-chair*)

Colin Yes. She's got a lot of the qualities Carol had in that respect. You're a lucky man, Paul.

Paul Yes. (*He sits in the armchair*)

Colin (*laughing suddenly*) It could have been me at one point, couldn't it? Remember? Diana and me instead of Diana and you.

Paul Could it?

Colin Oh, come on, you haven't forgotten that. (*To the others*) We were both after her—him and me—at one time.

Marge Were you really?

Colin Oh, yes. And I think it's fair to say, isn't it, Paul, fair to say, that there was one moment in time when I don't think she could honestly choose between us.

Marge Really, I didn't know.

Colin Still, it all ended happily, didn't it? Lucky old Paul and if I'd married Di, I wouldn't have met Carol . . .

Marge Yes.

Pause

Colin Talking of Carol, it's an odd thing you know. I'm sure this is fairly common. I mean, you read about it happening but there are times when I feel that she's still around somewhere. Some part of her. Her spirit or whatever you call it. She could be in this room at this moment. Odd, isn't it?

Marge It does happen to people. My Aunt Angela . . .

Colin I mean, I know for certain in my mind that she's dead. There's no doubt that she's dead. I saw her lying there dead with my own eyes . . .

John rises and jiggles about

But nevertheless, as I say, I feel that here, around here somewhere she's watching us. She can't communicate but she's watching me. Taking care of me.

John (*moving to the door*) Excuse me.

Marge All right, John?

John Yes, I'm just going to see if—Di's all right . . .

John goes out to the kitchen with the sandwich plate and his own side plate

Colin Good old John. He still can't sit still, can he?

Marge No.

Colin You took on a real live wire there, Evelyn.

Evelyn Oh yes?

Colin How do you manage to keep up with him?

Evelyn I don't bother.

Colin You'll have to get up early in the morning to catch John.

Evelyn I do. Every morning. He doesn't wake up at all unless I wake him.

Colin Oh well, that's marriage.
Evelyn How do you know?
Colin Well, I mean . . .
Marge Evelyn . . .
Evelyn What?
Marge Don't be so . . .
Evelyn What?
Marge Never mind.
Paul How long had you known Carol, Colin?
Colin Just over a year. Fourteen months, twenty-three days.
Paul Ah well. Time would have told.
Colin Told what?
Paul I mean, well—I mean, to be fair you hadn't time really to get to know
her. Not really.
Colin I think I knew Carol better than I've ever known anybody before
or since, Paul.
Paul Oh. Well. I'm sure . . .

Diana enters with a jug of cream

Diana I'm so sorry, everyone. I just wanted to make sure I'd turned the gas
off. Now this is the cream for the trifle afterwards if anybody wants any.
I've left that out there in the cool till we've cleared away some of this.
Oh, good you've started the sandwiches.
Marge Yes, I hope you didn't . . .
Diana No, no. They're there to be eaten.
Colin I'm very sorry, Di, if I upset you with—what I said . . .
Diana Oh no, Colin, no. Not at all. John's outside checking on the baby,
Evelyn.
Evelyn Oh.
Diana He thought one of you should. He's wonderful with that baby,
Colin. You should see him.
Colin I bet.
Diana (*sitting on the sofa*) Does all the things a mother should and better.

*Evelyn clicks her tongue. She picks up the magazine and buries her nose in
it rudely*

Colin (*rising*) You all right, Evelyn?
Evelyn Eh?
Colin (*moving to Evelyn*) Anything the matter? You seem a bit down.
Evelyn No. No. No . . .
Marge It's just her manner.
Diana You get used to it eventually.
Colin Oh. Do you know something, Evelyn? Now I'm talking off the top
of my head now because I've only just met you, I don't really know you
—but—I think Paul will back me on this, won't you, Paul—I've always
had this knack—gift if you like, I suppose you could call it—for being
able to sum people up pretty quickly. Sometimes I've just got to meet
them, exchange a few words with them and on occasions, not always but

on occasions, I know more about that particular person than they
know about themselves. Now, I could be wrong, as I say this is straight
off the top but I would say just from the brief time I've had to study
you, I would say something's bothering you. Right or wrong?

Evelyn Right.

Colin There you are. Now, I'm going to go a bit further and I warn you
I'm going to stick my neck right out now and say one of your worries
is John. Right?

Evelyn Amazing.

Colin (*moving round, then sitting on the upstage bar-stool*) No, not altogether. You see, I think I know what it is—(*to the others*)—excuse me,
I'm just putting Evelyn straight—right. Number one. John is a very high
powered individual—can't sit still, always on the move. We all know
him in this room very well. Probably better than you do, Evelyn. You
see, we've known him for years. He's an extrovert, good brain, clever—
wonderful with his hands. The sort of fellow, if you're in trouble, it's
John you go to. John is number one. Never let you down. The bee's
knees. But—and there's a big but—and I think everyone here will agree
with this—Marge, Di, Paul, Gordon if he was here—what we, everyone
of us have always said about John is—God help the woman he marries.
Because every day of their lives together, she is going to have to get used
to the fact that John is going to be the driver while she is going to have
to spend most of her life in the back seat.

Colin pauses for effect and gets one

(*Rising*) So. My advice is, don't let your personality—because I can see
there's a lovely personality hiding under there—don't let that get buried
away. Because he won't thank you for it in the end. Nobody will. Get
in the habit of giving yourself to people, if you know what I mean and
you'll get a lot more back, believe me. I'm a giver. It's natural, how I
was born, nothing virtuous about it, *per se*—just the way I'm made.
Others have to work at it. Carol was another giver. She'd give you
everything. Everything she had.

Silence

Marge True. True . . .

Colin Sorry. I'm preaching. I can feel it. Sorry, Evelyn. Beg your pardon.
I just happen to be an expert on John, that's all. I'm an expert on Paul
here as well. Shall I tell you about Paul?

Evelyn No thanks.

Colin No. Better not. He gets embarrassed.

Diana (*rising*) Yes. Another sandwich, everyone?

Colin Oh, ta. (*He sits on the sofa*)

John enters from the garden

Marge Is he all right?

John Yes. Fast asleep now.

Colin Just been talking about you.

John Who has?
Evelyn Him, mainly.
Colin Me, mainly.
John Oh.
Marge Yes, now we know, don't we, everyone?
Evelyn We certainly do.

Pause. Diana sits on the sofa after handing the sandwiches. Everyone settles.
John sits on the hearth bench

Colin Memory test. Do you remember, does anyone remember the last time we were all together like this? I mean as a group. If you count Gordon and don't count Evelyn. Does anyone remember?
Diana No. When would that have been?
Paul Dick's anniversary.
Colin No, no. Months after that.
Marge I give up.
Colin Do the words Stately Home remind you of anything?
Diana Stately Home? You mean that place?
John That place, yes . . .
Paul Oh, grief . . .
Marge The one day of the year we chose . . .
Diana And it's closed.
Marge That was dreadful, wasn't it?
Paul Proper waste of petrol.
Diana And then the rain.
Marge All that rain.
Diana And that was the day I lost that glove.
Marge Yes. That's it. And then Gordon lost the convoy. We were driving up here, down there, trying to find you.
John It was all right for you. We were sitting in that lay-by for two hours while you were seeing the countryside.
Colin Yes, but it was a marvellous day, wasn't it?
John Was it?
Colin Oh, it was a great laugh—sorry, Evelyn, this must be very boring for you, love . . .
Evelyn Yes.
Colin Remember that fabulous picnic?
Diana All I remember is running from one car to the other in the rain with the thermos flask.
Colin And we found a great place for tea.
Paul Where they overcharged us.
Colin It was great. I'll always remember that.
John Yes.
Colin What a marvellous day that was.
Diana (*doubtfully*) Yes.
Marge I suppose so, yes.
Colin You missed something there, Evelyn.
Evelyn Sounds like it.

Pause

Colin Poor old Gordon. Lying in bed while we're scoffing ourselves.
Marge Yes, shame.
Colin Now, Gordon's the opposite to John, isn't he? He's what, shy. I'd
call him shy, wouldn't you, Marge?
Marge Well, sometimes—yes. I suppose he has been.
Colin Big men are like that. They're always shy.
Paul I'm not shy.
Diana You're not very big.
Paul I'm fairly big.
Marge You're not as big as Gordon.
Paul Nobody's as big as Gordon.

Pause

Marge That's because I feed him. When his stomach's not playing him up.
Colin Gordon was famous for his appetite.
Marge He still is. I like a man with an appetite.
Colin There you are, you see. Two more satisfied customers.

Pause. Colin laughs

Diana What?
Colin Sorry. No, I was just remembering something.
Diana What?
Colin It was just something me and Carol—it wouldn't interest you.
Diana Go on.
Colin No, no . . .
Marge Go on. We want to hear about her.
Colin Well, it was just one of those fantastic moments, you know.
Marge (*romantic*) Ah . . .
Colin It was—well—when we first knew each other and—I forget where it
was now—I think we were walking across the common—there was no-
body about—and she suddenly turned to me and she said, "Colin, I
think I'm ready to let you kiss me now. I'd like that very much. Would
you, please."
Marge Ah . . .
Colin And after I'd kissed her, I remember I was over the moon, literally.
You should have seen me, I was singing and dancing and leaping about
all over that common . . .
Marge Ah . . .
Diana Ah . . .
Evelyn Huh.

Slight pause

Paul Have you given any thought as to who's going to win the League
this year, Colin?
Colin No, not really, no.
Paul I rather fancy our lot this year. They're going rather well . . .
John They are.
Colin Well, I still follow them. What was it? Four nil last Saturday. Did
you go?

Paul No. Yes.
Colin Sounded a cracker.
Paul It was.
Diana There's nothing much can come between Paul and a football game, is there, Paul? Now come on, I want all these eaten up or I won't cut the cake. (*She holds out the sandwiches*)
Marge (*rising*) Well, if you've got any left I'll take it home to Gordon in a bag. (*She takes a sandwich and moves to the pouffe*)
Paul Oh my God.
Colin It's a wonderful spread, Di. Really wonderful. Right up to standard.
Diana Thank you.
Colin Di's teas. Famous. I remember having a few of those over the years. Don't you, Paul?
Paul Eh?
Colin Remember when we used to go round to tea? To Di and her sister Barbara's?
Paul Oh yes.
Colin Every weekend. Mind you, Paul was in such a state, he could never eat it though. He'd say to me, how the hell am I supposed to sit down opposite a fantastic looking girl like that and be expected to eat anything. That's the last thing on my mind. He really had it bad.
Diana For Barbara?
Colin Barbara? Come off it. For you.
Diana Oh.
Paul No, I didn't.
Colin Look he's shy. He's gone shy. Big men, I told you. Tell her about the table napkin.
Paul Shut up.
Colin All right. I'll tell them. We used to go round to tea, you see, to their house—did I ever tell you this, John?
John Don't think so.
Paul Look, Colin . . .
Diana Shut up, Paul, I want to hear.
Marge We want to hear.
Colin I think it was, well, practically the first time we went round to Barbara, Di and her mother's for tea and Paul was—well, he was sweating—literally sweating and all the way there, he kept saying—what am I going to say to her—this was to Di. And when we got there, the girls and their mother had laid out this tea, all properly, you know. Table napkins, everything correct . . .
Paul Look, this was a long time ago.
Colin That's why I'm telling them.
Diana Shut up.
Colin (*rising*) Anyway, the first thing that happens, Paul and I are in the front room there, waiting—they're all out in the kitchen, giggling away, getting the tea ready—and Paul, well you know what he can be like, he gets so nervous, he's pacing up and down, sits down, gets up, sits down and then finally, he leans against the wall with one hand—like this, you see—(*he demonstrates*)—and he puts his hand right on one of these

ducks. China ducks, you know, the sort people have flying up their wall. A row of them, you know. Anyway, he puts his hand on one of them and crack—bang goes one duck. So there he is, he's standing there with half a duck in each hand and we hear them coming back. No time to do anything. So he sits down to tea with his pockets full of duck.

They all laugh

(*Sitting again*) There we are, sitting all through this tea waiting for someone to look up and say—hallo—one, two—what's happened to him. He must have migrated.

They all laugh again

Diana We never missed it.
Colin No, well. He took it home, glued it together and hung it up again when we came next week.
Diana Typical.
Colin He was so worried, he could hardly keep his eyes on Di. Anyway, at the end of the meal, do you know what he did—and this shows how romantic he is underneath all that lot—he picked up that napkin that you'd been using, Di, and he put it in his pocket. Took it home to remind him of you.
Marge Ah.
Diana Is that where it went.
Paul I don't remember doing that.
Marge I think that's a lovely story. Just shows. All men are romantic at heart.

Pause

John (*rising*) I never did that sort of thing.
Evelyn You nicked my uncle's screwdriver.
John I did not.
Evelyn He saw you taking it. He said if he comes round here again, I'll break his neck.
John You never invited me for tea.
Evelyn You never sat down for long enough.

John sits on the upstage bar-stool

Diana Now then. More tea?
Colin Please.
Paul (*laughing suddenly*) You know something, Col?
Colin What?
Paul I've just remembered. I've still got that table napkin of hers, you know.
Colin Have you really?
Paul Yes. I use it to clean the car with.

Diana rises, picks up the cream jug and pours it slowly over Paul's head. Paul sits for a moment, stunned

(*Leaping up*) Hey! What are you doing, woman?

Marge ⎡Di! ⎤ *Speaking*
Colin (*standing*)⎨ Hey, hey! ⎬ *together*
John ⎣Oy! ⎦

Diana Oh, I'm so sorry.

Paul (*outraged*) What are you doing?

Diana I am so sorry.

Paul You poured that all over me. She poured that over me.

Marge I'll get a cloth.

Paul No, I can't use a cloth. (*Moving to the stairs*) I'll have to wash it out.

Marge (*rising*) Not for you. For the chair.

Marge goes out to the kitchen

Paul Bloody woman's off her head. She poured it all over me.

Paul stamps off upstairs

Diana Accidents will happen.

Colin Well . . . (*He laughs awkwardly*)

Diana I'm sorry, Colin. You were saying? (*She sits in the dining-chair*)

Colin Was I?

Diana You'll have to excuse my husband, Colin, he's changed over the years . . . Now then, tea for you, John?

John Er—thank you.

Diana Pass your cup. Evelyn?

Evelyn No.

Diana Thank you.

Evelyn Thank you.

John brings his cup to Diana

Colin Well, I dare say we've all changed in some ways.

Diana Possibly. Some more than most.

Marge returns with a cloth, bowl of water and paper towels

Marge Would it be all right to use this for it, Di? (*She indicates the cloth*)

Diana Just as you like.

Marge Look, paper towels. Very useful. (*Examining the damage*) Oh, it's not too bad.

Marge sets to work. Diana pours tea for Colin

Diana Is that strong enough for you, Colin?

Colin Oh, that's lovely, Di. That's perfect. Perfect. (*Laughing*) Just the way Carol used to make it. (*He sits again*)

Diana (*pouring tea for John*) You can't say fairer than that, can you.

Colin Listen Di . . .

Diana John . . .

Slight pause. John takes his tea back to his seat

Colin Listen, Di . . . Just now, I think what Paul said just now—it may
have sounded to you a bit—er—well—I think, actually, I understand
what he was feeling. I know what was going through his mind. I embarrassed him with that story—I shouldn't have told it and—er—well,
Paul, basically—here I go again. I told you I'm a Paul expert . . .
Diana So am I, Colin. So am I.
Colin Yes, right, point taken, surely. But—you see, Paul is really a very
romantic man. He's soft. I've known him a long time—oh, he'll give you
that old gruff bit—and the "I don't care what anyone thinks" bit—but,
honestly, Di, you know yourself, he's ashamed of his own nature, you
see. Somewhere he's got this idea that, if he shows any sort of gentleness
to people, they'll think he's soft. And of course, that's what's made him
the success he is today. Let's face it. Because he's managed to cover it
up. And I think, that in some ways, you'd be the first to say thank
heavens he has. I mean. You've got this marvellous house, full of lovely
things, you've got two fine children and—well, let's be fair, you've got
just about everything a human being could ask for. And it's a very very
sad fact of life that you don't get any of that through being soft. That's
why people like me, John, Gordon, we're never going to get in the same
bracket as Paul. Never. No, Di, I'm afraid the only thing left for you is
to love him for what he is. Right, John?
John Right. Right.
Colin Marge?
Marge (*not quite convinced*) Yes . . .

Pause

Evelyn Do you happen to write for these magazines by any chance?
Colin Eh?

Pause. Marge finishes her task

Marge I think that's done it. Shall I do over the rest while I'm here, Di?
(*She laughs*)

Marge goes out with the cloth, bowl and towels

John You pleased with that car of yours?
Colin Yes. Yes, it gets me about.
John I've always fancied the look of those. The only thing that worries
me about it is, is it slightly under-powered?
Evelyn I bet it's got a carpet that fits.
Colin No, it seems to be okay. It's not a racer—but . . .
John No, no, quite. I think I'll consider getting one sometime.
Evelyn A cheap one with no wheels.
John Oh lay off, Evelyn. There's a good girl. I spend my days slaving for
her—slaving . . .

Marge enters

Marge There we are. All done. I think I've earned a spot more tea,
haven't I, Di?

Diana is in a trance of her own

Di?

Diana It's all yours.

Marge Oh, righto.

Marge pours herself a cup of tea

Diana (*quietly at first*) When I was a little girl, you know, my sister Barbara was very jealous of me because Mother bought me this coat for my birthday . . .

Marge Oh, really? (*She sits in the armchair*)

Diana I'd seen it in the window of this shop when I walked to school. It was red with one of those little collars and then trimmed round the neck and the sleeves. I used to pass it every day. They'd put it on this window dummy. A little child dummy. It was a really pretty dummy. Not like some of them. A proper face. It had very very blue eyes and sort of ash coloured hair, quite short and it was standing in the middle of this sort of false grass. I wanted that coat so much. And Barbara used to say, you'll never get Mother to buy you that. But I did. And on my birthday, I put it on and I felt, oh, so happy you can't imagine. And then we were all going for a walk and we were just going out and I happened to catch sight of myself full length in the mirror in the hall. And I looked like nothing on earth in it. I looked terrible.

Marge Oh dear.

Colin What a shame.

Diana Yes, it was. I wanted a red one especially. Because I had this burning ambition, you see, to join the Canadian Royal Mounted Police.

Marge Good gracious . . .

Diana People used to say, "You can't join the Mounted Police. You're a little girl. Little girls don't join the Mounted Police. Little girls do nice things like typing and knitting and nursing and having babies." So I married Paul instead. Because they refused to let me join the Mounted Police. I married him because he kept asking me. And because people kept saying that it would be a much nicer thing to do than—and so I did. And I learnt my typing and I had my babies and I looked after them for as long as they'd let me and then suddenly I realized I'd been doing all the wrong things. They'd been wrong telling me to marry Paul and have babies, if they're not even going to let you keep them and I should have joined the Mounted Police, that's what I should have done. I know I should have joined the Mounted Police. (*Starting to sob*) I want to join the Mounted Police. Please . . . (*She starts to sob louder and louder till they become a series of short staccato screams*)

Marge (*rising*) John, for heaven's sake. Get Paul down here.

Colin rises and retreats into a corner

John Paul. Yes, I'll get Paul . . .

John exits upstairs

Evelyn rises and studies Diana with curiosity, moving in towards her

Evelyn What's the matter with her?
Marge Get out of my way. (*Shaking Diana*) Di—Di—Di . . .

> *Paul enters, with John behind him. Paul's hair is still wet from his washing*
> *it*

Paul What's wrong? What's the matter with her?
Marge She's not well, Paul. You'll have to get a doctor.
Paul Di—Di, come on now . . .
John Shall I get her some water?
Paul No, we'll get her up to bed. We'll get a doctor. Give me a hand, John.
John Right.
Marge I'll get a cold cloth. That'll help.

> *Marge runs out to the kitchen*

> *John and Paul try to lift Diana by each arm*

Diana (*fighting Paul away*) Get away from me . . .
Paul Now, Di . . .
Diana Get away!
Colin (*ineffectually*) Can I . . .?
Evelyn I'll do it. Here.

> *Evelyn takes hold of Diana's arm, the one that Paul has relinquished. John*
> *still has hold of the other arm*

Diana (*thrusting Evelyn away with some violence*) Get away from me, you
bitch . . .

> *Marge enters with a flannel*

John It's no good. She won't let anybody—(*struggling with Diana*)—help
her.
Marge Here, hold this. (*She thrusts the flannel into Colin's hand*)
Colin Wah!
Marge Come along, out of the way.
John We could try slapping her face.
Marge No, we couldn't. How would you like your face slapped? Don't
be silly. Come along, Di, that's it . . .

> *Marge and John between them start to steer Diana to the door*

Colin Can I be of any . . .?
Marge It's all right, Colin, sit down. Easy with her, John, that's it. I'll
phone the doctor from upstairs, Paul.
Paul Right.
Marge You're still with Harris, aren't you?
Paul Yes.
Marge Come along, John. She needs support. Support her.
John I'm trying to support her. She's bloody heavy.

John, Diana and Marge go out upstairs

A silence. The men stand awkwardly. Evelyn sits in the armchair and picks her nails

Paul What started that?
Colin I don't really know. She just started talking about the Mounted Police. (*He sits on the sofa*)
Paul The what?
Colin The Royal Canadian Mounted Police. She seemed to want to join them.
Paul (*shaking his head*) Well . . . (*He sits on the dining-chair*)
Colin There's something very wrong there, Paul. Very wrong indeed.

Marge enters busily

Paul Can you manage?
Marge It's all right. She's just been a little bit ill on the stairs. Nothing serious. Evelyn.
Evelyn What?
Marge Paper towels. In the kitchen. Come on, this is partly your fault. You get them and clean it up.

Marge goes out. Evelyn clicks her tongue and goes off into the kitchen

Colin Have you had this trouble before, Paul?
Paul Not quite like this.
Colin Worrying.
Paul Right.
Colin I think you should go up with her, you know. She probably needs you.
Paul Oh, come on, Colin . . .
Colin What?
Paul You heard her. She doesn't want me within twenty yards of her.
Colin Oh, yes, but that was—she was hysterical. I mean . . . .
Paul I'm the last person.

Evelyn enters from the kitchen clutching a handful of paper towels

Evelyn This is a right cheery afternoon this is. His lordship's bawling his head off out there as well . . .

Evelyn goes off upstairs

Colin I remember when Carol had 'flu. She wouldn't let go of my hand. Except to turn over. I sat with her for two nights in a row. But then I think the thing with Carol and me was . . .
Paul Col.
Colin Yes?
Paul Do me a favour. Just shut up for one minute about Carol, would

you. I don't want to hurt your feelings but—not just at the moment . . .
Colin Oh, I'm sorry. I was—just thinking it—might help, you know.
Paul No, Colin. Really and truly, I don't honestly think it does. I mean, you and Carol were—something quite different, weren't you?
Colin Yes, I realize that, yes. (*He thinks for a moment*) All the same, you're wrong, you know.
Paul How come?
Colin Di didn't mean that. That she didn't want you near her.
Paul She convinced me.
Colin (*laughing*) No, no I'm sorry, Paul, you're not fooling anyone, you know. Neither's Di. Remember me? I'm the one that used to sit and talk to her for days and nights on end in the old days. Do you know what we talked about, constantly and incessantly?
Paul (*wearily*) Go on, amaze me . . .
Colin You. All you. I mean, at one time, when she used to ask me round a lot, I used to think, Hallo, I'm on to a good thing here. Can't be bad. Must mean something. And we'd sit down all evening, in her front room, drink coffee and talk about you all the time. Well, after a bit, I began to get the message. It wasn't me she was after at all. You . . . Only you were out with her sister Barbara. No, you're number one in Di's book, Paul. Always have been. I don't think you realize quite what a pedestal that woman has set you upon. She'd follow you to the ends of the earth, you know.
Paul She probably would at that.
Colin I hope you realize what you've got there?
Paul I do, I do.
Colin Stick with it, Paul, old mate.
Paul Thank you, Colin. Thank you very much.
Colin I know you will. I know you. (*Pause*) You know something? The one regret I'll always have? That Carol and I—our relationship—can never develop now into the sort of relationship you and Di must have . . .
Paul Oh, Colin . . .
Colin Never mind. Too late now. You feeling a bit brighter?
Paul Oh Colin, what are we going to do with you?
Colin Me? (*He laughs*) That's the last thing to worry about. Mind you, I'm glad I came round this afternoon. I don't know how you lot ever managed without me, eh?

Colin laughs. Paul laughs. Colin stops laughing. Paul continues. It's hysterical, almost manic, uncontrollable laughter. Colin becomes concerned

Evelyn enters. She stares at Paul

Evelyn What's the matter with him?
Colin He's—er . . . He's just . . .
Evelyn Oh. I'm going to fetch Wayne in. It's raining . . .

Evelyn goes out through the kitchen

Paul finally stops laughing

Paul I'm sorry, Col. Sorry . . . (*He rises*)
Colin All right?
Paul Yes, yes . . . (*He moves away*)

John enters from the stairs

John Right. Marge gave her one of her sleeping pills. If that doesn't get her to sleep, she says she'll phone the doctor.
Paul Thanks.
John Not at all, not at all. (*Looking around*) Has she gone home?
Paul No, she's with the baby.
John Ah. Sorry about that, Col old mate.
Colin Oh . . .
John Doesn't happen every day.

Paul sits in the armchair

Colin I hope not.
John You must come to our house next time. Absolute peace. Neither of us ever says a word to each other. That's the secret of a successful union. Marry a strong silent woman like Evelyn. (*He shadow-boxes*) Bam—bam . . . (*At the table*) Isn't anyone going to finish these?
Paul Help yourself.

John munches a sandwich

Colin (*taking a sandwich*) I must be off- soon, Paul. Don't want to be in the way, you know.

Paul, brooding, makes no reply

John (*munching*) The good thing about Evelyn—and she has her good side, although she is most careful to hide it from strangers—is that she has absolutely no sense of humour. Which is very useful since it means you never have to waste your time trying to cheer her up. Because she's permanently unhappy. Misery is her natural state. We are also fortunate in being blessed with a very miserable baby. In fact, apart from me, we are the most miserable family you are ever likely to meet and I'm working on me. Am I keeping you awake?
Paul Sit down.
John (*sitting on the dining-chair*) What do you think about that deal? Worth a try.
Paul I don't know.
John A hundred and twenty-five per cent. Worth a try.
Paul I'll think about it.

The phone rings

Answer that will you, John?
John (*doing so*) Hallo . . . Could you speak up? . . . Gordon? Hallo, Gordon, matey . . . It's John, yes . . . Yes, she's here . . . Wait a minute . . . I'll give her a yell.

Colin (*moving to the stairs*) I'll call her.
Paul Tell her she can take it upstairs.
John (*still listening at the phone*) Hang on, Col, she's here . . . You got it
  then, Marge—okay. She's got it . . . (*He goes to place the receiver and
  then, covering the mouthpiece, listens in. He laughs*)
Paul Put it down.
John (*enjoying himself*) Hang on, hang on.
Colin Tell her I'd like a word with him when she's . . .
John (*laughing*) He's burst his hot-water bottle. (*He listens*) He's in a
  shocking state.
Paul Put it down.
John You should hear . . .
Paul It's private, put it down.

John replaces the receiver reluctantly

Colin I wanted a word with him.
John I don't think you would at the moment. He's a moaner, isn't he?
  A real moaner. Big fat moaner. Old gloom Gordon.
Colin He was a great left-arm bowler.
John Oh, yes. Could have played for the County.
Colin Easily.
John Till he wrecked his shoulder.
Colin Tragic, that.
John Yes. We could do with a good left-arm bowler in this County.
Colin He had his heart set on that as a career, didn't he?
John Yes. What is he now? Fire prevention officer, married to Marge and fat.
Colin I think she's very good for him, don't you?
John Yes, she's all right. I don't know how good he is for her, though.
  (*He lifts the phone off the hook to listen for a second*)
Paul (*wearily*) What are you doing?
John (*laughing*) He's shouting his head off at her still. (*He stays listening
  and pulls a face at what he hears*)
Colin (*moving to him*) John—excuse me—do you mind? Thank you . . .
  (*He takes the phone from John*)
John (*startled*) What are you doing?
Colin (*into phone*) Hallo—hallo—Marge . . . Gordon. Sorry if this is a
  private conversation—pardon me for butting in—Colin here . . .
  Hallo, Jumbo . . . Excuse me, Marge . . . Just wanted to say, get well
  soon—pecker up, I expect Marge'll be home to look after you shortly,
  won't you, Marge? You've got a real treasure there, Gordon, a real
  treasure . . . God bless—won't talk any longer. Back to nurse Marge . . .
  Bye-bye—bye-bye, Gordon. (*He replaces the receiver*) That's nice.
  Managed a quick word, anyway. (*He smiles*)
Paul Oh, my God . . .
John How was he? (*He sits on the dining-chair*)
Colin Between you and me, I don't think he's too good. Marge sounded
  very cut up. Very cut up indeed.

Evelyn pushes the baby in

John (*rising*) You bringing him in?
Evelyn It's raining out there.
John Rain won't hurt him. Good for him. Make him grow.
Evelyn He's nearly off again, anyway.
Colin May I have a look?
Evelyn Yes. Just don't make daft noises at him. He doesn't like it.
Colin (*looking into the pram*) Oh, great. He's so—small, isn't he?
Evelyn Yes. Look at him, little devil, he's really fighting to stay awake.
Colin He's just great. The feeling you both must have, looking at him—
must make you so . . .
Evelyn (*cutting him short*) He's not bad. (*She rocks the pram. To John*)
We're going in a minute. (*She sits on the downstage bar-stool*)
John Right.
Colin (*sitting on the dining-chair*) Yes, as soon as Marge comes down, I
think I must . . .
John You all right, Paul?
Paul Fine. I must go up in a minute. I've got a lot of work to do, upstairs.

Marge comes in, blowing her nose

Marge She's nearly off to sleep. I think she'll be all right when she's rested.
Colin (*rising*) Ah, yes. Sleep. A great healer. (*Confidentially*) Hope you
didn't mind me butting in on the phone call just now, Marge
Marge That's all right, Colin.
Colin Thought, as he was on, I'd have a quick word with Gordon . . .
Marge Lovely.
Colin He sounded a bit—er—under the weather . . .
Marge He's all right.
Colin Not his usual cheery old self.
Marge He's all right.
Colin Sounded as if he could do with a bit of jollying up . . .
Marge (*more sharply*) He'll be perfectly all right the minute I get back to
him, don't worry, Colin. (*She sits on the sofa*)
Colin Ah, well. That's good. (*He sits on the dining-chair*)

*Paul sits with his eyes closed. Evelyn rocks the pram. John gazes out at the
garden. Marge sits wrapped in thought*

Well. (*Pause*) I suppose I ought to be . . . Much as I'd like to . . . Making
tracks and all that. (*Pause*) Yes. (*Pause. Looking at his watch*) Good
heavens, yes. Look at the . . . It's a long drive. I'd better make a start.
(*Pause*) Good-bye, all . . . (*He rises*)
Marge (*coming out of her reverie*) Oh, Colin, are you off? (*She rises*)
Colin Yes, I think I'd . . .
Marge Yes. Don't forget your photographs.
Colin Oh, no. I wouldn't do that. Not likely to do that.
Marge I hope you—manage all right, Colin.

Paul dozes off to sleep

Colin Me? Oh, I'm fine. I've always fallen on my feet, you know. I've

still got a good job—health and strength—and lately, I think I've found a few good friends over there, as well. Carol's parents, to name but two. I'm always round with them these days. You know, talking over old times and things. And if I really get a bit depressed, out come the old albums. It's a pity you didn't meet her, Marge. You'd have got on like a house on fire.
Marge Yes, I'm sure.
Colin Well. (*He goes to Evelyn*) Good-bye, Evelyn. Been a great pleasure meeting you.

Colin shakes Evelyn's hand

Evelyn Bye.
John Cheerio, old Col. See you.
Colin You bet. Come over and see me.
John Might just do that. When I get the new car. Have a few—(*drinking gesture*)—together.
Colin Any time. Paul. (*He wakes Paul up*)
Paul Bye, Colin. Take care.
Colin And you. Say good-bye to Di, will you.
Paul Oh, sure. She'll be sorry she missed you.
Colin Bye-bye, Marge. No, it's all right, I'll see myself out. (*Hesitating*) Er—I really appreciated you all inviting me over here, this afternoon, you know and, well—thanks a lot. You've really been great. All of you.
Marge Good-bye, Colin. And I hope, perhaps, you know—later on— you'll . . . once you've got over . . . I mean, I know it will be difficult for a time for you to forget about Carol . . .
Colin Forget her? Oh, come on, Marge. You know me better than that, don't you? (*Smiling round*) Bye-bye, all.

Colin goes out

Marge (*after a pause*) He's a nice boy, isn't he?
John Good old Col. Just the same.
Marge (*sitting on the sofa*) Paul. I'll have to go home to Gordon in a minute.

John sits on the hearth bench

Paul Yes. Fine, Marge. Fine. You do that . . .
Marge But if by any chance you need help—with her—you know my number. As soon as I've cleaned Gordon up, I can easily look back.
Paul No we'll manage, Marge, honestly.
Marge She should sleep now.

Evelyn starts singing, still rocking the pram. Paul starts to doze

John I'll cut that carpet up for the car tomorrow.
Marge I don't think I'd better leave Gordon on his own again when he's ill, you know. He doesn't like it. He prefers it if I'm there. (*Slight pause*) Oh, it's terrible, I haven't got the energy to move now. Once I've sat

down . . . I think those shoes will go with that coat. I hope so . . . oh, look at us. Honestly. All drooping about like wet weekends . . . still, why shouldn't we, I say. There are worse ways of spending the time. Than sitting peacefully with your friends. Nice to sit with your friends now and again. Nice . . .

Evelyn continues her singing. Marge daydreams. Paul starts to snore loudly. John jiggles. After a long pause—

the CURTAIN *falls*

FURNITURE AND PROPERTY LIST

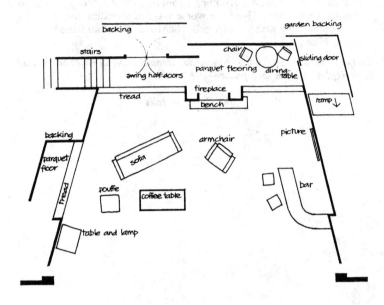

ACT I

On stage: Sofa. *On it:* cushions
Armchair
Pouffe
2 bar-stools
2 dining-chairs
Dining-table
Occasional table. *On it:* lamp
Hearth bench. *On it:* **Diana's** handbag with coins, cigarettes, lighter, matches, paper handkerchief; empty cigarette packet, sandwiches on plate, telephone
Bar. *On it:* plate of sandwiches, magazines, box of panatella cigars, ashtray, lighter, matches, toy, tray with drinks and glasses
Coffee table. *On it:* 7 cups, saucers and teaspoons, 2 large plates of sandwiches, 1 plate of brown bread, 1 plate of white bread, 1 plate of small cakes and biscuits, 1 plate of cake, 6 sideplates with 6 paper napkins, sugar bowl, sugar spoon, jug of milk. All food plates covered with paper napkins
Pram. *In it:* large doll camouflaged as baby with blankets and covering, noisy rattle stretched across front of pram, cassette recorder with continuous recording of baby crying. The latter is set alongside the "baby", so placed as to enable **John** to switch it on on cue, apparently adjusting the blanket
On walls: paintings, including one over bar

Off stage: Ashtray **(Diana)**
2 carrier bags. *In one:* general shopping. *In other:* shopping, paper-towel holder, shoes in shoe-bag **(Marge)**
Large handbag with knitting, pattern, comb, paper handkerchiefs **(Marge)**
Mats for teapot and hot water jug **(Marge)**
Teapot **(Paul)**
Hot water jug **(Marge)**
Large chocolate-box with album of photos and ten loose ones **(Colin)**

Personal: **Diana:** wristwatch
Evelyn: handbag, chewing-gum
Paul: wristwatch, towel
John: wristwatch, cigarette lighter with no fuel in it
Colin: wristwatch

Off stage: Jug of cream **(Diana)** Note: this can be made from a small part of a block of shaving soap. This is flaked then mixed with water in an electric blender, The temperature and time between mixing and use may affect the consistency of the mixture, which for best results should be roughly the consistency of thick double cream
Cloth, bowl of water, paper towels **(Marge)**
Damp flannel **(Marge)**
Paper towels **(Evelyn)**

COFFEE TABLE ARRANGEMENT

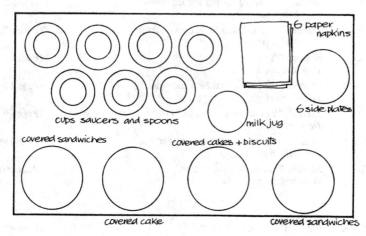

LIGHTING PLOT

Property fittings required: wall brackets, table lamp (dressing only)
Interior. A living-room. The same scene throughout

ACT I. Mid-afternoon
To open: General effect of afternoon light
No cues

ACT II. Immediately following
To open: As Act I

Cue 1   **Paul:** "I'm the last person."   (Page 43)
          Start slow fade of exterior lighting to ½

EFFECTS PLOT

ACT I

Cue 1   **Diana:** ". . . some feeling for me. Well."   (Page 3)
          Doorbell rings

Cue 2   **Marge:** ". . . to listen to you any further."   (Page 13)
          Doorbell rings

Cue 3   **Evelyn:** "Yes."   (Page 13)
          Doorbell rings

Cue 4   **Marge:** "Wouldn't that be a nice idea?"   (Page 18)
          Telephone rings

Cue 5   **Marge:** "You'll have to wash."   (Page 19)
          Doorbell rings

Cue 6   **Paul:** ". . . I could perhaps answer you."   (Page 19)
          Doorbell rings

Cue 7   **Marge:** ". . . but on the pillow."   (Page 20)
          Doorbell rings

ACT II

Cue 8   **Paul:** "I'll think about it."   (Page 45)
          Telephone rings